Made in the USA
Las Vegas, NV
05 December 2022

61093746R00063

This Book Belongs To:

____

Cock Coloring Book For Adults

Disclaimer

Fuck Off

I'm Coloring

Dicks